GOLDEN GATE

PHILIPPE FRANCQ • JEAN VAN HAMME

9th CINEBOOK
The 9th Art Publisher

With the authors' consent, and in order not to upset our more sensitive readers, certain illustrations of this edition of *Largo Winch* have been modified. The original version of *Largo Winch* is published in French by Dupuis.

Original title: Golden Gate

Original edition: © Dupuis, 2000
by Francq & Van Hamme
www.dupuis.com
http://www.largowinch.com

English translation: © 2010 Cinebook Ltd

Translator: Luke Spear
Lettering and text layout: Imadjinn
Printed in Spain by Just Colour Graphic

This edition first published in Great Britain in 2011 by
Cinebook Ltd
56 Beech Avenue
Canterbury, Kent
CT4 7TA
www.cinebook.com

A CIP catalogue record for this book
is available from the British Library

ISBN 978-1-84918-069-6

9th CINEBOOK
The 9th Art Publisher

DON'T COME ANY CLOSER, SHADOW! YOU GOT THE MONEY?

THERE IS NO MONEY, BARNEY, AND YOU KNOW IT, 'CAUSE IT WAS HER HUSBAND WHO HIRED YOU TO KIDNAP MRS TREVELEYAN HERE.

A JOKER, EH? THEN, TOO BAD FOR HER, SHADOW. AND TOO BAD FOR YOU.

I DON'T THINK SO, BARNEY. TREVELEYAN WAS ARRESTED AN HOUR AGO.

YOU SEE, TREVELEYAN MADE TWO MISTAKES. THE FIRST ONE WAS TO HIRE ME TO FIND HIS WIFE...

... AND THE SECOND WAS TO TAKE MIKE SHADOW...

... FOR A FOOL!

AAGHH

AAAHHH!

3

GET OUTTA HERE!

OW!

COME ON, DOLL, WE'RE LEAVING. THE COPS WILL BE HERE IN 10 MINUTES.

MY EYES... IT HURTS...

IT'LL PASS...

... IT'S BETTER THAN BEING CHEWED UP BY THE SHARKS IN THE BAY.

AND YOU SAVED ME! OH, MIKE, YOU ARE AMAZING!

I KNOW. TELL ME, BABY, DO YOU STILL HAVE THAT BUNGALOW ON THE BEACH? THE ONE WITH THE BIG BED?

MY... MY HUSBAND REALLY WANTED TO HAVE ME KILLED BY THOSE BRUTES?

AFFIRMATIVE. AND, AS IT HAPPENS, INHERIT YOUR FORTUNE. BUT I PUT A STOP TO HIS SCHEME.

COMPLETE TRASH!

A Candid Films / W9 Production

POOR SIMON. HE CAN'T ACT TO SAVE HIS LIFE.

HOW DID HE END UP IN THE LEAD ROLE OF THIS SERIES?

I HAVE NO IDEA, BUT THAT'S NOT MY BIG CONCERN, MR WINCH. I'LL TELL YOU WHAT'S ON MY MIND...

THIS JUNK, MADE BY W9*, OUR MAIN TV NETWORK ON THE WEST COAST, HAS 26 EPISODES PLANNED OF 42 MINUTES EACH, SIX OF WHICH HAVE ALREADY BEEN FILMED. ALL THE ACTION IS SUPPOSED TO TAKE PLACE IN SAN FRANCISCO IN THE '30S.

*WINCH 9

OF COURSE, MY DEPARTMENT RECEIVED THE FINANCIAL PLANS FOR "GOLDEN GATE." THE BUDGET IS $6 MILLION PER EPISODE, OR $156 MILLION TOTAL. THAT'S FOUR TIMES THE NORM FOR THIS KIND OF SERIES.

WHO'S PAYING?

AN INDEPENDENT PRODUCER FROM RENO, NEVADA—CANDID FILMS—THIS APPARENTLY BEING THEIR FIRST FORAY INTO A TELEVISION PROJECT. HE ALSO SUPPLIES SCRIPTS AND TAKES CARE OF CASTING. OUR NETWORK'S ROLE HAS BEEN LIMITED TO FILMING, EDITING AND, OF COURSE, BROADCASTING.

IN THAT CASE, APART FROM THE ABYSMAL RESULTS, WHAT'S THE PROBLEM?

HERE: THIS CLAUSE OF THE CONTRACT WITH CANDID FILMS STATES THAT HALF THE MONEY MUST BE IMMEDIATELY TRANSFERRED TO AN ANONYMOUS BANK ACCOUNT IN THE CAYMAN ISLANDS. SUPPOSEDLY TO PAY THE AMAZING SCRIPTWRITERS FOR THE SERIES.

AH... LAUNDERING DIRTY MONEY?

NO, IT'S THE OPPOSITE, BECAUSE THIS IS OFFICIAL MONEY TURNING INTO BLACK-MARKET MONEY. IT LOOKS MORE LIKE A TAX EVASION SCHEME. ANYWAY, I'VE SENT OUR INVESTIGATOR FROM THE NETWORKS DIVISION OVER TO TAKE A CLOSER LOOK...

HMMM... PRETTY GIRL.

AND ONE HECK OF A MIND. AN MBA** FROM HARVARD, MAGNA CUM LAUDE.

WASHINGTON, Sarah
Age: 29
Place of birth: Albany (N.Y.)

NOT BAD. HAS SHE FOUND ANYTHING?

I HAVE NO IDEA SARAH WASHINGTON SEEMS TO HAVE DISAPPEARED FIVE DAYS AGO! ③

**MASTER OF BUSINESS ADMINISTRATION

WHAT'S THE SITUATION WITH W9, MR COCHRANE?

THROUGH YOUR LIECHTENSTEIN COMPANY, YOU'RE A 55% SHAREHOLDER.

THE REMAINING 45% IS HELD BY NED BAKER, THE OWNER OF THE NBN*, OUR MAIN COMPETITOR ON THE WEST COAST, WHOSE HEADQUARTERS ARE LOCATED IN THE HEART OF SAN FRANCISCO. BAKER IS A FORMIDABLE TYCOON WHO OFFERED TO BUY W9 FROM YOUR FATHER SEVERAL TIMES.

*NED BAKER NETWORK

WHICH NERIO ALWAYS REFUSED, I PRESUME.

NATURALLY. HIRING COMPETITORS' MANAGERS IS COMMON PRACTICE IN THE UNITED STATES, PARTICULARLY IN TELEVISION.

EXCUSE ME FOR DISTURBING YOUR FLIGHT, GENTLEMEN...

OF COURSE. THE PROBLEM IS THAT, IN RECENT YEARS, W9 HAS BEEN LOSING MONEY IN THE FIGHT FOR RATINGS WITH NBN.

WALDO BUZETTI, THE PRESIDENT OF OUR NETWORKS DIVISION, HAS HIRED A NEW MANAGER, EARL QUINN, TO FIX THE SITUATION.

AND, NATURALLY, THIS QUINN CAME FROM NBN?

... BUT I'D ADVISE YOU TO PUT ON YOUR SEATBELTS. WE'VE JUST HEARD ABOUT A SPOT OF TROUBLE GATHERING OVER THE ROCKIES.

ALLOW ME TO REMIND YOU THAT THE FLIGHT SICKNESS PILLS CAN BE FOUND IN THE FIRST AID KIT BEHIND THE BAR AND THAT THERE ARE PARACHUTES UNDER THE BEDS AT THE BACK OF THE PLANE.

HOW'S IT LOOKING?

ANGRY. FORCE 10 OR 11 WIND, MAGNETIC STORM AND PLENTY OF TURBULENCE. ALL THAT IN QUITE A SHORT WEATHER FRONT.

CAN'T YOU AVOID IT?

CAN'T GO DOWN BECAUSE OF THE MOUNTAINS, AND THEY SAY THE STORM CEILING IS ABOVE 30,000 FEET. HERE, LOOK AT THIS WHILE YOU WAIT FOR THE ROLLER COASTER. I BOUGHT IT BEFORE WE LEFT.

Star

September 14, 1989 $2.50 Canada $3.50

Fall TV preview

ENEY COX'S EDDING

BEST & WORST DRESSED

SHANNEN DOR... W...

F... ON THE WEDDIN

Simon O' Vronnaz is Mike Shadow in GOLDEN GATE
a new series being shot in San Francisco by W9

GOOD OL' SIMON! LOOKS LIKE HE DIDN'T DO TOO BADLY WHILE YOU WERE PLAYING CONDOTTIERE IN VENICE.

ME NEITHER. I HEAR THE GIRLS ARE SOMETHING ELSE.

AH, HERE IT IS. TIME TO ROCK AND ROLL! HAVE YOU BEEN TO CALIFORNIA BEFORE, LARGO?

NEVER.

THAT'S WHAT THEY SAY.

YOU STILL IN CONTROL?

I'VE SEEN WORSE, ALTHOUGH YOUR MOWGLI JET'S GETTING A LITTLE OLD.

THE ONLY PROBLEM IS THAT THE RADAR...

110

NAV

TEST

130.5

WHOA! DON'T PEOPLE PAY FOR THIS KIND OF FUN AT DISNEYLAND?!

SO WHAT'S ALL THIS ABOUT SIMON PLAYING BOGART IN BORSELLINO?

HAVEN'T GOT THE SLIGHTEST IDEA. IT'S SOMETHING I'VE BEEN WONDERING ABOUT.

CANDID FILMS, THE COMPANY THAT FINANCES THIS SERIES, BELONGS TO A CERTAIN CANDIDO PANATELLA FROM CUBA. HE HAS THE BIGGEST CASINO IN RENO.

SO WHAT?

SO, NOTHING. I SMELL A RAT, THAT'S ALL.

YOU'LL SOON HAVE IT FIGURED OUT. WE'RE OUT OF THE TURBULENCE NOW, AND IN 45 MINUTES WE SHOULD BE LANDING IN FRISCO.

EASY, MR COCHRANE. YOU'LL BE OKAY. WE'RE HERE NOW.

WELCOME TO CALIFORNIA, MR WINCH.

EARL QUINN. DID YOU HAVE A GOOD FLIGHT?

EXCELLENT. JUST A BIT OF TURBULENCE OVER THE ROCKIES. ISN'T THAT RIGHT, MR COCHRANE?

GRUMBLE...

8

MR OVRONNAZ APOLOGISES FOR NOT COMING TO WELCOME YOU, BUT THE FILMING HAS TIRED HIM...

... WE'VE JUST FINISHED THE SEVENTH EPISODE AND I'VE GIVEN THE WHOLE TEAM A REST FOR ONE DAY.

I UNDERSTAND. THE LIFE OF A CELEBRITY MUST BE TERRIBLY STRESSFUL.

ABSOLUTELY. TO ALLOW MR OVRONNAZ TO RELAX BETWEEN SHOTS, WE RENTED HIM A SMALL VILLA JUST OUTSIDE OF TOWN.

VERY MODEST, INDEED.

HERE WE ARE.

9

HEY, LARG, MY MAN!...

IT'S GREAT THAT YOU CAME. DID YOU SEE? I'M LEARNING TO SWIM.

I SAW.

I ALSO SEE THAT YOU'VE GROWN A BELLY, SIMON O'VRONNAZ.

THAT? PFFT... JUST A LITTLE PADDING. TWO OR THREE MASSAGES AND IT'LL BE GONE.

CHERRY-LEE, MY TREASURE, BE A LOVE AND TAKE US TWO HOUSE COCKTAILS TO THE WEST TERRACE.

RIGHT AWAY, SIMON-PIE.

WHAT DO YOU THINK OF THE PAD?

HARDLY WORTHY OF YOUR TALENT... SIMON-PIE.

I HAVE A DRIVER, A COOK, A PERSONAL MASSEUSE AND... COMPANY. THIS IS REAL LIVING, MY FRIEND!

I CAN IMAGINE, SURE. HOW DID THIS FAIRYTALE START?

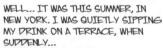

WELL... IT WAS THIS SUMMER, IN NEW YORK. I WAS QUIETLY SIPPING MY DRINK ON A TERRACE, WHEN SUDDENLY...

EXTRAORDINARY!...

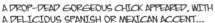

A DROP-DEAD GORGEOUS CHICK APPEARED, WITH A DELICIOUS SPANISH OR MEXICAN ACCENT...

YOU ARE EXACTLY THE MAN I'VE BEEN LOOKING FOR. COULD YOU GET UP, PLEASE?

ME??

THAT'S RIGHT. WHAT DO YOU DO, MR...?

ERM... OVRONNAZ, SIMON OVRONNAZ WELL... I DO A LITTLE BIT OF THIS AND THAT...

EXCELLENT.

ARE YOU MARRIED?

NOT AT THE MOMENT.

PERFECT. COME WITH ME. I'VE RESERVED US A TABLE AT CLUB 56.

YOU'VE JUST MET THE OPPORTUNITY OF YOUR LIFE, MR OVRONNAZ.

AND THE NEXT DAY, I WAS ON THE PLANE WITH A CONTRACT IN MY POCKET. BUT I'D BEEN HAD: JUST $200,000 PER EPISODE. AFTER THE SUCCESS OF THE FIRST SERIES, I'LL ASK FOR A MILLION.

FOR A STAR, THAT'S THE MINIMUM.

SHLRRRP...

AND WHAT HAPPENED TO HER, YOUR HIDDEN-TALENT-DISCOVERING FAIRY GODMOTHER?

FLOR DE LA CRUZ?

YOU'LL SEE HER TOMORROW ON SET. SHE'S CANDID FILM'S EXECUTIVE PRODUCER. OF COURSE, YOU'RE STAYING HERE, LARGO...

I'VE PREPARED A ROOM FOR YOU... WITH AN EXTRA OF YOUR CHOICE, IF YOU SEE WHAT I MEAN.

I SEE VERY WELL, SIMON. VERY, VERY WELL.

LISTEN, STAR, I MADE MY WAY OUT HERE TO SAY HELLO TO YOU BECAUSE YOU WERE TOO TIRED TO COME TO THE AIRPORT. BUT COCHRANE AND I WOULD PREFER TO STAY IN A HOTEL. THANK YOU FOR THE DRINK AND I'LL SEE YOU TOMORROW.

OH?...

SO, TO SUM UP, MR QUINN...

OUT OF THE SIX MILLION THAT CANDID FILMS IS GIVING YOU PER EPISODE, YOU ARE TRANSFERRING THREE TO AN ANONYMOUS CAYMAN TRUST LTD. BANK ACCOUNT, PLUS $500,000 THAT YOU TRANSFER TO PANATELLA'S PRIVATE ACCOUNT IN RENO AS PRODUCER'S SALARY. IS THAT RIGHT?

THAT'S RIGHT. WHICH LEAVES ME $1.5 MILLION FOR SHOOTING AND A $1 MILLION BONUS.

SO, FOR 26 EPISODES, $26 MILLION NET PROFIT TO FILL THE W9 COFFERS, WHICH DESPERATELY NEED IT.

AND THIS FINANCING PROCESS DOESN'T SEEM ODD TO YOU?

OF COURSE IT DOES, BUT IT'S NOT MY PROBLEM. I'M HAPPY TO RESPECT THE CLAUSES OF A COMPLETELY LEGAL CONTRACT.

WHO OWNS THE ACCOUNT IN THE CAYMAN ISLANDS, MR QUINN?

I HAVEN'T GOT THE SLIGHTEST IDEA. IT SHOULD BE THE SERIES' SCRIPTWRITER. I ONLY KNOW HIS CODE NAME: SHADOW. JUST LIKE THE HERO OF OUR SERIES, WHICH ISN'T COMPLETELY LACKING IN IRONY.

HMM... DO YOU KNOW WHAT HAPPENED TO SARAH WASHINGTON, MR QUINN?

SHE SPENT TWO DAYS AT THE W9 HEADQUARTERS GOING OVER THE ACCOUNTS. THEN SHE WENT TO SEE PANATELLA IN RENO, AND I HAVEN'T HEARD FROM HER SINCE. WHY? HAS SHE DISAPPEARED?

MY OPERATIONAL INVESTIGATORS HAVE TO SEND ME A REPORT EVERY DAY. I HAVE RECEIVED NOTHING FROM MS WASHINGTON FOR A WEEK.

PERHAPS SHE WAS TAKEN OVER BY THE GAMBLING DEMON. ANYTHING'S POSSIBLE IN RENO OR LAS VEGAS.

INCLUDING THE WORST. I ABSOLUTELY WANT TO STOP THE FILMING OF THIS SERIES, MR QUINN.

⑩

??

MAY I ASK WHY?

BECAUSE IF THE OWNER OF THIS ACCOUNT IN THE CAYMAN ISLANDS TURNS OUT TO BE AN AMERICAN CITIZEN, W9 WOULD BE SUBJECT TO PROSECUTION FOR INVOLVEMENT IN TAX FRAUD. APART FROM THE FACT THAT THIS SERIES IS TURNING OUT TO BE EVEN MORE CATASTROPHIC THAN THE WORST B-MOVIE.

YOU'VE NOT READ THE CONTRACT CORRECTLY, MR WINCH...

LOOK AT AMENDMENT 2: IF FILMING IS HALTED BEFORE THE 26TH EPISODE IS FINISHED, W9 SHALL NOT ONLY REIMBURSE THE COMPLETE FINANCING, $156 MILLION, BUT PAY CANDID FILMS AN ADDITIONAL CANCELLATION FEE OF $50 MILLION. DO YOU THINK THAT OUR NETWORK HAS THE MEANS TO PAY OUT OVER $200 MILLION, MR WINCH?

DID YOU KNOW ABOUT THIS CLAUSE, MR COCHRANE?

IT'S NOT IN THE COPY OF THE CONTRACT THAT I RECEIVED.

THIS AMENDMENT WAS SIGNED OFF LATER. MY SECRETARY MUST HAVE FORGOTTEN TO SEND YOU A COPY.

LET'S BE CLEAR, WINCH. I WAS HIRED TO TURN AROUND YOUR NETWORK'S FINANCES, AND THAT'S JUST WHAT I'M IN THE PROCESS OF DOING, FOR GOD'S SAKE! WHETHER OR NOT "GOLDEN GATE" IS A DOG OF A SERIES BROADCAST AT 3AM IS THE LEAST OF MY WORRIES. WHAT COUNTS IS THE $26 MILLION IT WILL BRING US.

AND I DON'T CARE IF PANATELLA IS A DRUG LORD, A MAFIA BOSS OR A NUCLEAR MISSILE TRAFFICKER, AS LONG AS I STAY ON THE RIGHT SIDE OF THE LAW.

YOU'RE FORGETTING ONE DETAIL, QUINN...

I AM THE MAJORITY SHAREHOLDER OF W9.

EXACTLY, AND YOU'LL FINALLY GET YOUR DIVIDENDS. YOUR FORTUNE MUST CERTAINLY GIVE YOU THE CARE-FREE SPIRIT OF A BOY SCOUT, WINCH, BUT THE TELEVISION WAR IS NOT A JAMBOREE.

IT TOOK ME SIX MONTHS TO PUT TOGETHER THIS PROJECT WITH CANDID FILMS. AND NOBODY, NOT EVEN YOU, WILL STOP ME FROM FULFILLING MY MISSION RIGHT TO THE END. THE FILMING OF "GOLDEN GATE" WILL CONTINUE, WHATEVER HAPPENS. GOOD NIGHT, GENTLEMEN!

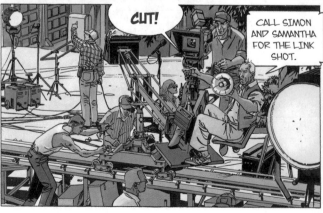

14

SIMON!...

SIMON!

SIMON!...

ATTENTION, EVERYBODY IN PLACE...

ENGINE!

THE CRASH!

GAS!

ACTION!

LOOKS LIKE YOUR PROBLEM IS SOLVED, DOLL. BUT WE'D BETTER BE SURE.

OH, MIKE, YOU'RE AMAZING!

I KNOW.

EXPLOSION!

VVROOUUUU

WHERE ARE WE GOING TO CELEBRATE, BABY? YOUR PLACE OR MINE?

CUT! WE'RE DOING THAT AGAIN RIGHT AWAY.

13

MARAVILLOSO!

SIMON!... SIIIMON!...

EEEEEE!

I'M GOING TO PASS OUT...

PLEASE, SIMO-O-O-O-N!...

FLOR, MY FAIRY GODMOTHER, WHAT A PLEASURE!

OH, SIMON, WHAT A GREAT ACTOR YOU MAKE!

LATER, MY DARLINGS, LATER. I'M BUSY NOW.

SIMON, PLEEEEASE...

SEE MY PRESS AGENT. SHE HAS SIGNED PHOTOS.

FLOR, MY BEAUTIFUL, ALLOW ME TO INTRODUCE MY FRIEND LARGO WINCH.

I RECOGNISED HIM. DELIGHTED TO HAVE YOU HERE WITH US, MR WINCH.

SO THIS IS THE FAMOUS TALENT SCOUT. PLEASURE TO MEET YOU, MISS DE LA CRUZ.

MR PANATELLA HAS ASKED ME TO ASK YOU IF YOU'D ACCEPT AN INVITATION TO DINE WITH HIM TOMORROW NIGHT.

IN SAN FRANCISCO?

RENO. MR PANATELLA IS OLD AND DOESN'T TRAVEL. I HAVE HIS PERSONAL HELICOPTER. AT MOST, IT WILL BE A ONE-AND-A-HALF-HOUR FLIGHT.

I'D BE QUITE CURIOUS TO MEET YOUR BOSS. I ACCEPT WITH PLEASURE.

ON THAT NOTE, I HAVE TO LEAVE YOU. SEE YOU TONIGHT, SIMON AND TAKE CARE OF YOURSELF—I THINK YOU HAVE A DANGEROUS JOB.

GIVE UP MY CAREER?!?... ARE YOU CRAZY?!?

WHAT'S GOT INTO YOU, LARGO? ARE YOU JEALOUS OF MY SUCCESS OR WHAT?

SEEMS TO ME THAT WE'RE PROBABLY BOTH VICTIMS OF A SCAM. I SMELL A RAT, SIMON.

ACT ONE: PANATELLA AND QUINN ARRANGE THE FINANCING OF A TV SERIES IN SUCH AN UNDERHANDED WAY THAT A BLIND PERSON COULD SEE IT FROM 100 MILES AWAY. SO, THE LOGICAL REACTION OF THE W GROUP'S ADMINISTRATOR IS TO SEND AN INVESTIGATOR TO TAKE A CLOSER LOOK. BUT THE INVESTIGATOR MYSTERIOUSLY DISAPPEARS.

ACT TWO: TO PLAY THE HERO OF THE SERIES, MISS DE LA CRUZ "DISCOVERS" A GUY WHO'S TOTALLY DEVOID OF TALENT BUT WHO HAPPENS TO BE MY FRIEND. AS FOR THE SCRIPT OF THE SERIES IN QUESTION, PROVIDED BY THE PRODUCER, IT IS ALMOST AS EXCITING AS THE EASTERN BELUCHISTAN PHONE BOOK.

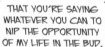

ACT THREE: AT THE LAST MINUTE, OUR TWO ACCOMPLICES SIGN AN AMENDMENT THAT STATES THAT IF FILMING HALTS, PANATELLA GETS HIS MONEY BACK AND RECEIVES AN ADDITIONAL FEE OF $50 MILLION. WHAT CONCLUSIONS DO YOU DRAW FROM THAT, SIMON?

THAT YOU'RE SAYING WHATEVER YOU CAN TO NIP THE OPPORTUNITY OF MY LIFE IN THE BUD.

UNTIL NOW, YOU'VE BEEN THE STAR, LARGO. THE YOUNG, HANDSOME BILLIONAIRE WHO ALWAYS WINS IN THE END. AND YOU DON'T LIKE THAT YOUR SIDEKICK HAS BECOME MORE FAMOUS THAN YOU. THAT'S WHAT CONCLUSION I DRAW.

THOSE HOLLYWOOD MASSAGES HAVE SOFTENED YOUR BRAIN, MY FRIEND.

THERE ARE TWO POSSIBILITIES FOR INTERRUPTING THE FILMING OF "GOLDEN GATE" AND THUS ALLOWING PANATELLA TO POCKET THE 50 MIL BONUS. THE FIRST IS FOR MR LARGO WINCH, MAJORITY SHAREHOLDER OF W9, TO ORDER IT. BUT QUINN DOESN'T WANT THAT, AS IT WOULD BE THE DEATH OF THE NETWORK.

THE SECOND IS THAT AN ACCIDENT HAPPENS TO THE STAR OF THE SERIES. DID YOU KNOW THAT QUINN HAS TAKEN OUT LIFE INSURANCE FOR YOU FOR $50 MILLION?

SO WHAT? THAT'S NORMAL FOR A STAR, ISN'T IT?

OF COURSE. SO, MR O'VRONNAZ JUST HAS TO DIE IN AN ACCIDENT FOR EVERYONE TO BE HAPPY BECAUSE THE INSURANCE WILL PAY 50 MIL RIGHT INTO PANATELLA'S POCKET. HAVE A GOOD NIGHT, STAR.

!??

16

LARG... WAIT A MINUTE...

ARE... ARE YOU SERIOUS?...

THINK ABOUT IT, SIMON. YOUR HEAD HAS A PRICE OF $50 MILLION; IT'S AS SIMPLE AS THAT. YOU SHOULD BE PROUD, RIGHT?

WELL, THEN, WHAT SHOULD I DO, DAMMIT?

CHANGE YOUR DRIVER AND HAVE HIM CHECK THE BRAKES OF YOUR LIMOUSINE EVERY DAY. HIRE ONE OR TWO BODYGUARDS. COOK WHAT YOU EAT YOURSELF, OR GO TO A RESTAURANT. DON'T GO INTO ANY BUILDINGS WITH MORE THAN TWO FLOORS. AND DON'T GO ANYWHERE NEAR WATER WITHOUT A LIFE JACKET.

OR, FORGET ABOUT IT AND COME BACK TO NEW YORK WITH ME.

BUT, IF I FORGET ABOUT IT... YOU SAID IT YOURSELF: YOUR NETWORK COULD GO BANKRUPT.

I KNOW. BUT I'D RATHER LOSE A COMPANY THAN A FRIEND.

BUT DON'T WORRY— NOTHING SHOULD HAPPEN TO YOU BEFORE THE 15TH OR 20TH EPISODE. THE LONGER FILMING IS CARRIED OUT, THE MORE MONEY PANATELLA WILL MAKE ON THE BACK OF W9.

IF YOU SAY SO....

WANT ME TO TAKE YOU BACK TO YOUR HOTEL?

NO, THANK YOU. I'D RATHER NOT TAKE UNNECESSARY RISKS. I'LL WALK.

DRIVE SLOWLY, DRIVER, VERY SLOWLY. MR O'VRONNAZ ISN'T FEELING VERY WELL.

MR WINCH?...

NED BAKER. GET IN, PLEASE. THE STREETS OF SAN FRANCISCO ARE NOT SAFE AT NIGHT. EVEN WHEN YOU'RE WEARING THROWING KNIVES AROUND YOUR ANKLES.

?

LUCKY GUESS, MR BAKER. AND I'M NOT TALKING ABOUT THE "LUCK" THAT BROUGHT YOU TO THIS AREA TONIGHT.

YOUR EXPLOITS ARE FAMOUS, MR WINCH. GET IN, PLEASE. WE HAVE THINGS TO DISCUSS.

I KNEW YOUR FATHER WELL, YOU KNOW. OLD NERIO WAS A TOUGH FIGHTER.

SEEMS SO. HOW DID YOU END UP WITH 45% OF W9, MR BAKER?

BY BUYING SHARES AT A GOOD PRICE FROM THOSE WHO HELD THEM, QUITE SIMPLY. MAINLY FROM THE EMPLOYEES OF YOUR NETWORK.

AND YOU'D LIKE TO GET HOLD OF THE REST, I SUPPOSE. THE REASON FOR THIS... DISCREET MEETING?

I REGRET TO INFORM YOU, MR BAKER, THAT I TEND TO ENJOY MY INDEPENDENCE. JUST AS NERIO ENJOYED HIS.

NATURALLY, I WAS EXPECTING THAT ANSWER. BUT THINK ABOUT IT. YOU KNOW HOW TO REACH ME IF YOU CHANGE YOUR MIND. GOODNIGHT, MR WINCH.

MR RUDI GESSNER, PLEASE. FOR LARGO WINCH.

JUST THE MAJORITY WOULD BE ENOUGH FOR ME, MR WINCH. W9 IS LOSING MONEY. BY MERGING IT WITH NBN, WE COULD REALISE SERIOUS ECONOMIES OF SCALE WHILE BECOMING THE FOURTH LARGEST NETWORK IN THE UNITED STATES. WHAT DO YOU THINK?

NOTHING RIGHT NOW.

DO WE HAVE A BANK IN THE CAYMAN ISLANDS? OF COURSE, LIKE EVERYBODY: THE WEST BAY SAVINGS BANK LTD.

DOES IT HAVE ANY LINKS WITH THE CAYMAN TRUST?

I THINK I REMEMBER THAT ONE OF THE ADMINISTRATORS FROM WEST BAY WAS ALSO A MEMBER OF THE BOARD FOR THE CAYMAN TRUST. WHY?

BECAUSE I'D LIKE TO IDENTIFY SOMEONE WHO HAS OPENED AN ACCOUNT UNDER THE CODE NAME SHADOW.

HMM... THAT WILL BE DIFFICULT. IN THE CAYMANS, THERE IS COMPLETE BANKING ANONYMITY, EXCEPT FOR DRUG MONEY. TO OPEN AN ACCOUNT OVER THERE, YOU DON'T NEED TO SUPPLY ANY IDENTIFICATION; A CODE NAME AND A PASSWORD ARE ENOUGH. UNLESS...

UNLESS WHAT?...

IN MOST TAX HAVEN BANKS, THE KEY CLIENTS ARE PHOTOGRAPHED BY HIDDEN CAMERAS. JUST IN CASE THEY WERE SUSPECTED OF BEING DRUG TRAFFICKERS.

GREAT. DO YOU THINK THAT YOUR ADMINISTRATOR COULD TRY TO FIND A PHOTO OF THIS SHADOW, IF THERE IS ONE?

I COULD ALWAYS ASK HIM TO TRY. I'LL LET YOU KNOW.

HAVE YOU WORKED FOR PANATELLA FOR A LONG TIME, MISS DE LA CRUZ?

THREE YEARS.

BEFORE THAT, I WORKED FOR CUBAN NATIONAL TELEVISION. DON CANDIDO GOT ME A VISA FOR THE USA TO CREATE HIS PRODUCTION COMPANY.

DON CANDIDO... SOUNDS A BIT MAFIA, DOESN'T IT?

DON'T START IMAGINING THINGS, MR WINCH. IN HISPANIC COUNTRIES, THE USE OF "DON" IS NOTHING OTHER THAN A MARK OF RESPECT. TO MANAGE HIS CASINO IN PEACE, DON CANDIDO IS FORCED TO HAVE A GOOD RELATIONSHIP WITH THE MAFIA, BUT THAT DOESN'T MEAN THAT HE'S PART OF IT.

OF COURSE, YOU HAD NO IDEA THAT HE WAS MY FRIEND?

ABSOLUTELY NOT. AND I DO RECOGNISE THAT IT IS ONE OF THOSE STRANGE COINCIDENCES THAT LIFE SOMETIMES THROWS AT US.

OK. WHY DID YOU HIRE SIMON, MISS DE LA CRUZ?

BECAUSE HE PERFECTLY FIT THE TYPE THAT WE WERE LOOKING FOR TO PLAY THE MIKE SHADOW CHARACTER.

HAVE YOU EVER BEEN TO RENO, MR WINCH?

NEVER.

THEN EXPECT TO BE SURPRISED. IT ISN'T AS WELL-KNOWN AS LAS VEGAS, BUT I CAN GUARANTEE YOU THAT YOU'LL HAVE MORE FUN...

... WHATEVER KIND OF FUN YOU'RE LOOKING FOR.

THERE THEY ARE. GO TO GREET THEM, ARTURO. AND MAKE AN EFFORT TO BE NICE FOR A CHANGE.

I'M AMAZED THAT A GROUP THE SIZE OF YOURS DOES NOT HAVE A HOTEL IN NEVADA, MR WINCH.

MY ADOPTIVE FATHER, NERIO, DISAPPROVED OF GAMBLING. FOR HIM, RENO AND LAS VEGAS WERE CITIES OF SIN.

THAT'S PROBABLY TRUE. BUT THE NORTH AMERICANS, WHO THINK THEY'RE SO VIRTUOUS, NEED TO SIN FROM TIME TO TIME TO KEEP THEIR BALANCE. COMING HERE IS LESS EXPENSIVE THAN THE PSYCHOANALYSTS' FEES.

IF YOU DON'T MIND, I HAVE A FEW QUESTIONS TO ASK YOU, DON CANDIDO. FOR STARTERS, DO YOU KNOW WHAT HAPPENED TO SARAH WASHINGTON, AN EMPLOYEE OF OUR GROUP WHO CAME TO SEE YOU A WEEK AGO?

FLOR SAID YOU'D ASK ME THAT.

ENQUIRIES HAVE BEEN MADE. THIS LADY SCHEDULED A MEETING WITH MY ACCOUNTANT. BUT SHE DIDN'T SHOW UP—THAT'S ALL I CAN TELL YOU. NEXT QUESTION?

WHY ARE YOU FINANCING GOLDEN GATE?

WHAT, FLOR DIDN'T TELL YOU? IT'S NOT CANDID FILMS WHO FUNDED YOUR SERIES, BUT A FINANCIER WHO WOULD LIKE TO REMAIN ANONYMOUS. HE HAS CHOSEN US AS EXECUTIVE PRODUCERS, AND WE RECEIVE $500,000 PER EPISODE TO PAY THE SCRIPTWRITERS, MISS DE LA CRUZ'S SALARY AND OUR ADMINISTRATIVE FEES. THAT'S ALL.

AH. AND TO TRANSFER HALF OF THE BUDGET TO THE CAYMAN ISLANDS?

ONE OF THE FINANCIER'S DEMANDS. DON'T ASK ME WHY. I HAVE NO IDEA, AND IT'S NOT MY PROBLEM.

YOU CAN EXAMINE CANDID FILMS' ACCOUNTS WHENEVER YOU LIKE, MR WINCH. APART FROM THE IDENTITY OF THE GOLDEN GATE BACKER, I HAVE NOTHING TO HIDE FROM YOU.

YES, DON CANDIDO?

I'LL ASK YOU TO EXCUSE ME, MR WINCH. I'M AN OLD, TIRED MAN AND FLOR HAS BROUGHT ME SEVERAL FILES THAT WE HAVE TO GO OVER TONIGHT. IT HAS BEEN A GREAT HONOUR TO MEET YOU.

OF COURSE, YOU ARE MY GUEST. JULIET WILL SHOW YOU THE GAMING ROOMS AND WILL TAKE YOU TO YOUR ROOM WHEN YOU ARE READY. SHE IS AT YOUR SERVICE FOR WHATEVER YOU WOULD LIKE.

JULIET, MY CHILD, TELL THE CHIEF CASHIER TO GIVE $10,000 IN CHIPS TO MR WINCH FROM ME SO THAT HE HAS SOMETHING WITH WHICH TO ENTERTAIN HIMSELF.

YES, DON CANDIDO.

OUR TRUTH.

GUANTANAMERA HAS FIVE GAME ROOMS, FIVE RESTAURANTS, 12 BARS, THREE NIGHTCLUBS, TWO THEATRES, FOUR SWIMMING POOLS AND 1,200 ROOMS. IT'S ONE OF THE MOST LUXURIOUS CASINOS IN RENO.

VERY IMPRESSIVE.

WHAT DO YOU THINK?

THAT HE'S HANDSOME...

... AND THAT, UNTIL NOW, HE HAS BEHAVED EXACTLY AS YOU PREDICTED.

CERTAINLY. BUT I KNOW THE BOY'S REPUTATION. HE IS CAPABLE OF THE MOST UNEXPECTED REACTIONS. KEEP AN EYE ON HIM, FLOR. IF REQUIRED, HELP HIM TO SEE THE TRUTH.

22

24

WHAT WOULD YOU LIKE TO PLAY, MR WINCH? SLOT MACHINES, BLACKJACK, BACCARAT, CRAPS, ROULETTE?

I'M NOT A GAMBLER, JULIET. NOT FOR GAMES OF CHANCE, IN ANY CASE.

LET'S SEE, MR WINCH. YOU HAVE $10,000 TO RISK. COME ON, LET'S PLAY ROULETTE; THAT'S THE MOST EXCITING.

IS IT TRUE THAT YOU'RE ONE OF THE RICHEST MEN IN THE WORLD? I READ AN ARTICLE ABOUT YOU IN A MAGAZINE.

27, RED, ODD AND 19 TO 36!

OH, THAT'S GREATLY EXAGGERATED. BILL GATES AND THE SULTAN OF BRUNEI BEAT ME EASILY.

YOU KNOW THE RULES, I SUPPOSE?

PLACE YOUR LADIES AND GENTLEMEN!

BETS,

VAGUELY. PUT EVERYTHING ON RED, JULIET.

EVERY-THING!?... ON RED!?

YES, PLEASE.

OK.

NO MORE BETS...

11, BLACK, ODD AND 1 TO 18!

THAT'S DUMB. YOU LOST EVERYTHING!

A SIMPLE RETURN TO SENDER, JULIET. COULD YOU TAKE ME TO MY ROOM? I'D LIKE TO TAKE A BATH AND MAKE A FEW CALLS.

IT'S ONE OF OUR BEST SUITES, WITH A SUPERB VIEW OVER THE CITY. A KING-SIZE BED, SAUNA, JACUZZI, WIDESCREEN TV, FREE MINIBAR, AND SLOT MACHINE IN THE BATHROOM. YOU CAN ALSO PLAY BINGO BY VIDEO.

WELL, NOW, JULIET, WHAT ARE YOU DOING?

COME ALONG, MR WINCH. THIS SUITE IS TOO BIG FOR ONE MAN ALONE.

BE KIND AND PUT YOUR CLOTHES BACK ON. I INTEND TO SLEEP TONIGHT.

WHY? DON'T YOU LIKE ME?

YOU'RE CHARMING, JULIET, BUT A LITTLE TOO YOUNG FOR ME. APART FROM THAT, I DON'T LIKE LOVE ON DEMAND. YOU'LL PASS MY APOLOGIES ON TO DON CANDIDO.

IF PANATELLA IS TELLING THE TRUTH, WHICH IS FAR FROM CERTAIN, WHERE CAN THIS MONEY BE COMING FROM? AND WHY? I'LL HAVE TO ASK COCHRANE TO TRY TO FIGURE OUT ITS ORIGIN.

I HAVE SOME GOOD NEWS AND SOME BAD NEWS FOR YOU, SARAH WASHINGTON. THE GOOD NEWS IS THAT YOUR GREAT BOSS, DEAR MR WINCH, CAME IN PERSON TO ENQUIRE ABOUT YOUR WELLBEING.

THE BAD NEWS IS THAT HE WON'T FIND YOU.

HHHHH- HHNG

IN TWO WEEKS, WHEN YOU HAVE BECOME MORE DOCILE, I WILL SELL YOU TO THE JAPANESE. IT SEEMS THEY LOVE WELL-ENDOWED BLACK GIRLS OVER THERE.

IN THE MEANWHILE, AS YOU MUST BE FEELING A LITTLE LONELY, I'VE BROUGHT YOU SOME COMPANY.

SWEET DREAMS.

KLAK

ARE THEY YOUR NEW BODYGUARDS?

YEAH.

ONE... HIC... AS DRIVER AND THE OTHER... HIC... FOR PERSONAL PROTECTION.

I THOUGHT WE WERE YOUR BODYGUARDS, SIMON-PIE...

YOU UNDERSTAND... HIC... AFTER WHAT THAT BASTARD LARGO TOLD ME, I HAVE TO... HIC... TAKE PRECAUTIONS.

WHY DON'T YOU JUST FORGET IT? LARGO'S RIGHT: YOU'RE A TERRIBLE ACTOR.

PFFT... YOU'RE SAYING THAT BECAUSE YOU'RE JEALOUS. FILMING ISN'T EVEN OVER YET AND I'VE ALREADY HAD MY PHOTO ON THE COVER OF THREE MAGAZINES. MY AUDIENCE WILL LOVE ME. ISN'T THAT RIGHT, GIRLS?

COMPARED TO YOU, MEL GIBSON IS RAT PISS.

OH, YES, SIMON-PIE, YOU'RE THE BEST!

AND THEN, YOU KNOW, FREDDY, I DON'T WANT TO FORGET IT... THE VILLA, THE LIMOUSINE, THE CASH, THE GIRLS... THESE KINDS OF THINGS ONLY HAPPEN ONCE IN YOUR LIFE.

ESPECIALLY WHEN YOUR LIFE IS AT RISK OF BEING SHORT.

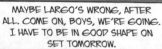

MAYBE LARGO'S WRONG, AFTER ALL. COME ON, BOYS, WE'RE GOING. I HAVE TO BE IN GOOD SHAPE ON SET TOMORROW.

YOU CAN LEAVE, SIR. THE COAST IS CLEAR.

SAY, FREDDY, DO YOU KNOW THE NUMBER TO THAT CHUMP COCHRANE'S SUITE?

OF COURSE. IT'S 815. WHY?

BECAUSE I HAVE AN OLD SCORE TO SETTLE WITH THAT STONE-COLD PRESBYTERIAN.

SO, HERE'S WHAT WE'LL DO. WE'LL START BY GOING INTO A 24-HOUR STORE AND THEN... ZZZZZZZZZZ... GOT THAT, GIRLS?

GOT IT, SIMON-PIE. BUT ONLY BECAUSE IT'S YOU.

LARGO WON'T LIKE THIS.

I DON'T CARE; HE'S NOT MY BOSS. WAIT FOR ME HERE, BOYS.

OK, BOSS.

LADIES? GENTLEMEN?...

DON'T GET UPSET, BUDDY. WE'RE JUST ACCOMPANYING OUR FRIEND UP TO HIS ROOM

YOU THINK YOU CAN...?

YOU'RE FORGETTING MY PAST, PILOT. NO LOCK HAS EVER RESISTED THE GREAT SIMON OVRONNAZ.

SURPRISE!!!

OVRONNAZ! WHAT DO YOU MEAN BY THIS INTOLERABLE INTRUSION!?

THAT YOU REALLY NEED TO PARTY, GOOD OLD DWIGHT. COME ON, GIRLS, TAKE CARE OF HIM!

LADIES, I FORBID YOU TO TOUCH ME!...

RELAX, MY BIG, STRONG WOLF.

YOU'LL GET ALL THE HUGGING YOU NEED.

OH, WHAT A BIG BED!

NO, DON'T...

GO ON, GO ON.

!

CAYMAN TRUST LTD

Code name:
SHADOW

Access code:
|

STOP!... I DON'T... NO...

RELAX, DWIGHT. IT'LL ALL BE A LOT BETTER WITH A LITTLE CHAMPAGNE. YOU'LL SEE...

HMMM GULP GULP GULP

SMILE, HANDSOME DWIGHT. I'M SURE MRS COCHRANE WILL LOVE THESE PHOTOS.

30

YOU KNOW, FREDDY, WE'VE KNOWN EACH OTHER FOR MANY YEARS, BUT YOU'VE NEVER TOLD ME HOW YOU MET LARGO.

THAT'S ANCIENT HISTORY, SIMON.

THEY'RE THE KIND OF STORIES I PREFER.

IF YOU WANT. BUT, THEN, WE MAY AS WELL START RIGHT AT THE BEGINNING. I WAS BORN IN A KIBBUTZ IN THE NORTH OF GALILEE, NEAR THE GOLAN BORDER. MY PARENTS WERE FROM UKRAINE AND HAD MANAGED TO EMIGRATE TO ISRAEL IN '53, AFTER STALIN'S DEATH. THEY WERE KILLED IN OCTOBER '73 WHEN THE SYRIANS STARTED THE YOM KIPPUR WAR.

I WAS 12 YEARS OLD, AND THAT DAY, I SWORE I'D KILL EVERY LAST ARAB IN THE WORLD.

AFTER THE WAR, I STAYED IN THE KIBBUTZ LIKE THE OTHER ORPHANS, RAISED BY THE COMMUNITY. AT 18, I WENT TO THE AIR FORCE OFFICERS SCHOOL, AND AT 25 I WAS A CAPTAIN, AT THE CONTROLS OF AN F-16B FIGHTER BOMBER.

ONE DAY, I WENT ON A MISSION TO BOMB A HIDDEN HEZBOLLAH CAMP IN SOUTHERN LEBANON. I WAS ESCORTED BY TWO ROCKET-LAUNCHING FALCON FIGHTERS. I FELT GOOD; I WAS FINALLY GOING TO GET MY ARABS.

THE MISSION WAS A COMPLETE SUCCESS.

SIX TONNES OF CLUSTER BOMBS, 12 ROCKETS AND FOUR AIR-TO-GROUND MISSILES RIGHT ON TARGET.

BUT WHAT THE ARMY'S INTELLIGENCE SERVICES DIDN'T KNOW IS THAT HEZBOLLAH'S MEN HAD LEFT THE CAMP THE NIGHT BEFORE, LEAVING ONLY WOMEN AND CHILDREN. MY BOMBING CAUSED 80 DEATHS AND OVER 300 INJURED...

THE INTERNATIONAL SCANDAL WAS ENORMOUS. TO COVER ITSELF, THE GENERAL STAFF CLAIMED THAT I HAD THE WRONG TARGET AND, UNDER PUBLIC PRESSURE, CONDEMNED ME TO THREE YEARS IN MILITARY PRISON.

OF COURSE, I WAS ALSO STRIPPED OF MY RANK. BUT I DIDN'T CARE ABOUT THAT. IN MY CELL, I COULDN'T STOP THINKING ABOUT THE WOMEN AND CHILDREN THAT I HAD KILLED, AND IT MADE ME SICK. WHAT I HAD SWORN IN 1973 SUDDENLY MEANT NOTHING. I HAD BECOME A BUTCHER.

SIX MONTHS LATER, I MANAGED TO ESCAPE AND LEFT ISRAEL BY FLYING A...?...

I'LL SAVE THE REST OF THE STORY FOR ANOTHER TIME. SWEET DREAMS, MIKE SHADOW.

SARAH WASHINGTON? IF SHE FILLED IN A HOTEL FORM, I SHOULD BE ABLE TO FIND IT FOR YOU.

THERE... SARAH WASHINGTON, THE NIGHTS OF THE 25TH AND 26TH, MONTROSE HOTEL, CARSON STREET. IT'S A SMALL, PEACEFUL HOTEL IN A RESIDENTIAL AREA.

THANK YOU FOR YOUR HELP, SERGEANT.

YES, I REMEMBER HER. IT'S RARE IN RENO TO HAVE A PRETTY GIRL ON HER OWN WHO'S NOT A WHORE. SHE SPENT TWO NIGHTS HERE BEFORE LEAVING FOR THE CAYMAN ISLANDS.

THE CAYMAN ISLANDS... ARE YOU SURE?

I CALLED WINCHAIR MYSELF TO BOOK HER TICKET. THEIR OFFICES ARE ON MAIN STREET.

INDEED, SIR. MISS WASHINGTON TOOK FLIGHT NUMBER 9452 ON THE 26TH FOR MIAMI, AND FROM THERE, FLIGHT 4210 FOR GEORGETOWN.

IT WOULD APPEAR THAT YOUR INVESTIGATOR IS IN THE CAYMAN ISLANDS, MR COCHRANE.

I KNOW. SHE'S JUST SENT ME AN E-MAIL FROM GEORGETOWN. I'LL READ IT OUT LOUD TO YOU...

"I THINK I'VE DISCOVERED THE TRUTH. I'LL NEED YOU OUT HERE BECAUSE THIS IS TOO BIG FOR ME. CAN YOU MEET ME AT THE SANDY BEACH HOTEL IN GEORGETOWN, GRAND CAYMAN? SARAH WASHINGTON."

I SUPPOSE THAT YOU'LL BE GOING?

I'M TAKING A FLIGHT THIS VERY MORNING. BESIDES, A CHANGE OF SCENERY WOULD BE GOOD FOR ME.

33

MR WINCH... I'VE BEEN LOOK-ING ALL OVER FOR YOU.

IF YOU'D LIKE TO GO BACK TO SAN FRANCISCO, WE'RE LEAVING IN HALF AN HOUR.

VERY WELL. I'LL JUST GET MY THINGS AND MEET YOU ON THE HELIPAD ON THE ROOF.

OF COURSE, IF YOU WANTED TO STAY A LITTLE LONGER, WE COULD DELAY OUR DEPARTURE FOR A DAY OR TWO. YOU'VE SEEN NONE OF THE HIDDEN PLEASURES OF RENO.

I WOULD HATE TO DEPRIVE THE FILMING OF OUR SERIES OF ITS EXECUTIVE PRODUCER, MISS DE LA CRUZ. SEE YOU IN HALF AN HOUR.

MR WINCH...

JULIET?...

QUICK, LET ME IN! NOBODY CAN SEE ME HERE.

WHAT'S GOING ON, JULIET? HAVE YOU BEEN HIT?

I WAS... PUNISHED BECAUSE I DIDN'T PLEASE YOU LAST NIGHT. THAT'S HOW IT WORKS HERE.

WHAT DO YOU MEAN? TELL ME MORE.

OH, MR WINCH, I BEG YOU... GET ME OUT OF THIS CITY AND HIDE ME FAR AWAY FROM HERE. I KNOW YOU CAN DO IT. IN EXCHANGE, I'LL TELL YOU EVERYTHING I KNOW ABOUT PANATELLA'S TRAFFICKING.

WHAT TRAFFICK-ING?

TRAFFICKING GIRLS, OF COURSE. DON CANDIDO RUNS THE BIGGEST PROSTITUTION NETWORK IN NEVADA.

BZZZ
BZZZ

FLOR, ONE OF MY MEN JUST SAW WINCH SLIP OUT THE BACK OF THE HOTEL WITH THAT LITTLE PUTA JULIET.

WELL, WELL... HOW LONG AGO?

TEN MINUTES.

SEND YOUR MEN TO WATCH THE TWO MAIN CITY EXITS IN CASE THEY HIRED A CAR. AND TELL OUR FRIENDS AT THE AIRPORT TO STOP THEM IF THEY SEE THEM THERE. I'LL TAKE CARE OF THE BUS STATION. MY INTUITION TELLS ME THAT THAT'S THE WAY THEY'LL TRY TO LEAVE.

IT'S THE BEST WAY TO LEAVE THE CITY, JULIET. SLOWER, BUT SAFER.

THEY'LL DEFINITELY BE WATCHING THE BUSES AT THE RENO EXITS. ARTURO, PANATELLA'S LIEUTENANT, HAS A WHOLE TEAM.

Greyhound

THAT'S PROBABLY LIKELY, BUT I DOUBT THEY'D TRY ANYTHING WHILE WE'RE SURROUNDED BY WITNESSES. IT'S OUR BEST FORM OF PROTECTION.

I'M AFRAID, MR WINCH. IF THEY CATCH ME, THEY'LL KILL ME. AND MAYBE YOU, TOO.

AREN'T YOU EXAGGERATING A LITTLE? THERE'S OUR BUS. YOU'LL BE SAFE IN JUST A FEW HOURS.

S. FRISCO

GREYHOUND

COME ON, GET ONBOARD! YOU'VE NOTHING TO FEAR.

BUT...

SEATING CAP. 55

GET ON, JULIET!

㉝

IF I WERE YOU, I WOULDN'T TAKE THAT BUS, MR WINCH.

?

GO BACK TO THE HOTEL, WINCH. OUR HELICOPTER'S WAITING FOR YOU. IT WILL BE LESS RISKY... THERE ARE SO MANY TRAFFIC ACCIDENTS NOWADAYS.

SORRY, FRIEND, BUT I PREFER THE BUS. I WANT TO DO SOME SIGHTSEEING ON THE WAY.

HEY, MAN! ARE YOU GETTING ON OR TAKING THE NEXT ONE?

SEE YOU IN SAN FRANCISCO, MISS DE LA CRUZ, PERHAPS.

THEY KNOW WHERE WE'RE GOING. THEY'LL DEFINITELY WAIT FOR US ON ARRIVAL. WHAT ARE WE GOING TO DO?

WE'LL IMPROVISE.

DID YOU FIND THEM?

THEY TOOK THE GREYHOUND FOR SAN FRANCISCO.

PERFECT. YOU KNOW WHAT TO DO.

③④ VAN HAMME & FRANCQ

SOME OF THE GIRLS IN PANATELLA'S NETWORK COME THROUGH EXCHANGES WITH OTHER NETWORKS IN ASIA AND LATIN AMERICA. BUT A LOT OF THEM COME TO RENO BECAUSE THEY WERE PROMISED WORK OR FILM STARDOM. BUT, ON ARRIVAL, THEIR IDENTIFICATION IS STOLEN, ALONG WITH THEIR MONEY AND ALL THEIR POSSESSIONS.

OF COURSE, NEARLY ALL OF THEM FIGHT BACK. SO, THEY'RE LOCKED IN CELLARS WHERE ARTURO'S MEN BREAK THEM EMOTIONALLY AND PHYSICALLY UNTIL THEY'D AGREE TO ANYTHING. I SPENT A WEEK IN THERE, AND IN THE END I WAS READY TO ACCEPT ANYTHING. THOSE WHO REFUSE TO GIVE IN DON'T MAKE IT OUT ALIVE.

THEN THEY'RE TOLD THE REAL REASON THEY'RE IN NEVADA: THE GAME. BEING FORCED TO BRING IN BETWEEN $500 AND $1,000 PER DAY ON PAIN OF PUNISHMENT. ARTURO MANAGES THE GIRLS. HE'S A MONSTER.

THE LUCKIER GIRLS, LIKE ME, STAY IN THE GUANTANAMERA, WHERE THEY HAVE TO SUBMIT TO ALL OF DON CANDIDO'S RICH CLIENTS' FANTASIES. THE OTHERS "WORK" IN OTHER CASINOS IN RENO OR VEGAS, IN CARS OR JUST OUT ON THE STREET, CONSTANTLY WATCHED BY ARTURO'S MEN.

NEARLY ALL THE GIRLS ARE FORCED TO PERFORM IN ADULT MOVIES. PANATELLA HAS A LARGE UNDERGROUND STUDIO IN THE DESERT, WITH ALL SORTS OF SETS. HE DOES MAINSTREAM ADULT MATERIAL BUT ALSO MORE SPECIALISED FILMS: S&M, BESTIALITY, ETC...

HAVE YOU BEEN THERE?

YES, AND IT'S A MEMORY I'D RATHER FORGET. I THINK THEY ALSO MAKE SNUFF MOVIES—VIDEOS WHERE THE GIRL IS TORTURED AND THEN STRANGLED, LIVE IN FRONT OF THE CAMERA.

IT'S FLOR DE LA CRUZ WHO MAKES NEARLY ALL THESE FILMS HERSELF. SHE LOVES IT; SHE'S REALLY SICK.

SOME HAVE, AND WE NEVER SAW THEM AGAIN. THE POLICE ARE INVOLVED; IT'S OBVIOUS.

THE GIRLS WHO SNITCH OR TRY TO ESCAPE ARE CONDEMNED TO THE SNUFF MOVIES. THE ONES WHO HAVE GOTTEN TOO OLD OR TOO MESSED UP BY A CLIENT, THEY'RE SENT TO SOUTH AMERICAN OR AFRICAN BORDELLOS, WHICH MUST BE EVEN WORSE THAN DEATH.

YOU NEVER THOUGHT TO GO TO THE POLICE?

WHEN I SAW YOU, I WAS SURE YOU COULD GET ME OUT OF THAT HELLHOLE, MR WINCH. SO, I TOOK THE RISK. AND NOW I'M SO SCARED.

YOU DID WELL, JULIET. I'LL GET YOU OUT OF THERE, I PROMISE.

SILVER CREEK JUNCTION! ONE-HOUR LUNCH BREAK!

STAY IN THE MIDDLE OF THE CROWD, JULIET. THEY CAN'T DO ANYTHING HERE.

THEY WON'T LET US GO, MR WINCH.

THAT'S OBVIOUS TO ME. DO YOU KNOW HOW TO RIDE A HORSE?

A LITTLE. I WAS BORN IN WYOMING. WHY?

THERE. I THINK WE'VE BEAT THEM. THEIR CAR CAN'T FOLLOW US INTO THE DESERT.

OH, MY GOD... LOOK OUT!!...

GRAA
RRRAAA

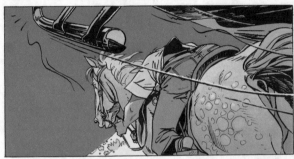

THEY'RE COMING BACK! WE'RE DONE FOR!

NO, WE'RE SAVED... LOOK!

40

THEY'RE LEAVING?

FLOR CAN'T RISK THE DRIVER SEEING HER REGISTRATION NUMBER.

BUT WE'RE NOT OUT OF THE WOODS YET. SHE'LL TELL ARTURO THE TRAIN'S SCHEDULE, AND HE'LL BE WAITING FOR US AT THE FIRST STOP. FORTUNATELY, GOODS TRAINS DON'T STOP VERY OFTEN.

THEN, WHAT WILL WE DO?

JUMP OFF WHEN THE TRAIN SLOWS DOWN FOR THE NEXT TOWN. THERE WE'LL FIND A RENTAL CAR TO GET TO SAN FRANCISCO BY THE BACK ROADS.

BUT THEY KNOW WE'RE GOING TO SAN FRANCISCO. THEY'LL FIND US EASILY.

THERE'S STILL A POPULATION OF ONE MILLION PEOPLE. I'LL RENT A SMALL, FURNISHED APARTMENT UNDER THE NAME OF MR AND MRS MAC LANE, A YOUNG MARRIED COUPLE, AND YOU WON'T LEAVE IT UNDER ANY CIRCUMSTANCES.

AND YOU?

I HAVE A FEW SCORES TO SETTLE; THAT WILL TAKE TWO OR THREE DAYS. THEN I'LL TAKE YOU TO ANYPLACE IN THE WORLD THAT YOU WANT. YOU'LL HAVE A NEW IDENTITY, OF COURSE. NOBODY WILL BE ABLE TO FIND YOU.

A YOUNG MARRIED COUPLE... THAT'LL MAKE ME FEEL ALL WEIRD.

HOW OLD ARE YOU, JULIET?

I'M 22. MR WINCH... SORRY, LARGO...

WOULD IT SHOCK YOU VERY MUCH IF A FUTURE EX-PROSTITUTE ASKED YOU TO KISS HER?

GOLDEN GATE 8, BLEEDING DOLL, 17/4, TAKE THREE.

HEAVENS, MY HUSBAND!

THE ELEVATOR'S OUT OF ORDER. HE'S COMING UP THE STAIRS. WHAT ARE WE GOING TO DO, MIKE?

RELAX, DOLL. EVERYTHING WILL BE OKAY.

ALL YOU HAVE TO DO IS UNHOOK THE ROPE WHEN I'M AT THE BOTTOM.

BUT, MIKE... WE'RE ON THE 15TH FLOOR!

COME ON, BABY! NEXT TO MIKE SHADOW, TARZAN AND KING KONG ARE NOTHING BUT TREE-HUGGING HIPPIES.

OH, MIKE, YOU'RE AMAZING!

I KNOW. HASTA LA VISTA, DOLL! AND GIVE MY BEST TO YOUR HUSBAND!

CUT! THAT'S GREAT. WE'LL KEEP IT.

DIDN'T YOU WANT A STUNT-DOUBLE FOR SUCH A DANGEROUS SCENE?

HEY, LARGO. WHERE WERE YOU YESTERDAY? WE WAITED FOR YOU.

I TOOK THE SCENIC ROUTE.

I'VE GOT SOME GOOD NEWS FOR YOU; YOU'RE NO LONGER AT RISK OF HAVING AN ACCIDENT. I'VE STOPPED FILMING.

?!?

40

BY WHAT RIGHT?...

BY MY RIGHT AS MAJORITY SHAREHOLDER OF W9. FILMING OF THIS SERIES WILL BE SUSPENDED FOR AS LONG AS I HAVE DOUBTS ABOUT THE ORIGIN OF ITS FINANCING. THIS DECISION IS FINAL.

WHERE IS YOUR BROTHER, GRACE? I NEED TO HAVE A SERIOUS CONVERSATION WITH HIM, BUT WE HAVEN'T SEEN HIM IN HIS OFFICE FOR TWO DAYS.

ERM...

I DON'T KNOW. I THINK HE WAS CALLED TO THE LOS ANGELES DIVISION HEADQUARTERS BY BUZETTI, BUT I'M NOT SURE.

THIS IS STUPID, LARGO. I WAS JUST STARTING TO GET INTO MY CHARACTER.

THEN I SUGGEST YOU GET OUT OF IT. STAY HIDDEN AWAY IN YOUR DREAM VILLA WITH YOUR GORILLAS AND YOUR PRETTY MASSEUSES, SIMON.

I'LL GET IN TOUCH WITH YOU WHEN I'VE FOUND OUT MORE.

IT'S ME, JULIET. LARGO.

I'VE BROUGHT YOU A FEW SUPPLIES. TOMORROW I'LL BRING YOU A CHANGE OF CLOTHES.

THANK YOU.

HAVE YOU SETTLED IN HERE?

I'M SCARED, LARGO.

HOW LONG WILL I HAVE TO WAIT HERE?

I TOLD YOU. TWO OR THREE DAYS. AS LONG AS WE'RE CAREFUL AND YOU DON'T SET ONE FOOT OUTSIDE, NOBODY WILL KNOW YOU'RE HERE.

YOU'RE LEAVING ALREADY? YOU'RE GOING TO LEAVE ME ALONE?

THERE'S A BOTTLE OF MILD SLEEPING PILLS IN THE BAG I BROUGHT YOU. TAKE ONE TONIGHT. IT'LL HELP YOU SLEEP. I'LL COME BY AGAIN TOMORROW MORNING TO SEE YOU. BE BRAVE, JULIET; SOON, THIS'LL ALL BE JUST A BAD MEMORY.

HAS HE GONE?

YES.

YOU WERE PERFECT, CHIQUITA. IF YOU WANTED TO, YOU'D MAKE AN EXCELLENT ACTRESS.

WHAT YOU MAKE ME DO IS DISGUSTING. THAT WINCH REALLY IS A GOOD GUY.

DON'T YOU WORRY ABOUT THAT, SWEETIE. KEEP DOING AS WE SAY AND YOU'LL GET YOUR FREEDOM. OTHERWISE, YOU KNOW WHAT'S WAITING FOR YOU.

DURING YOUR LITTLE ESCAPADE, YOU DIDN'T TELL HIM TOO MUCH ABOUT OUR ACTIVITIES, I HOPE?

N... NO, OF COURSE NOT!

I... I WAS SO SCARED WHEN FLOR SHOT AT US FROM THE HELICOPTER...

THAT HAD BETTER BE TRUE, CHIQUITA. IF FLOR REALLY WANTED TO KILL YOU, SHE WOULDN'T HAVE MISSED. YOU CAN BE SURE OF THAT.

GET UP!

OK, LET'S START THE NEXT PART OF THE OPERATION. ARE YOU READY?

ERR... YES.

PERFECT.

AH, MR WINCH... I HAVE TWO MESSAGES FOR YOU. ONE FROM MR COCHRANE...

... AND A PHOTO THAT WE RECEIVED ONLINE FROM THE GRAND DUCHY OF LUXEMBOURG.

THANK YOU, GEORGE. COULD YOU GET ME A LIGHT MEAL? I HAVEN'T EATEN ANYTHING SINCE THIS MORNING.

"S.W. NOWHERE TO BE FOUND IN GEORGETOWN. BACK TO S.F. TOMORROW. COCHRANE."

RRiiNGG RRiiNGG ...

I RECEIVED A PHOTO OF YOUR SHADOW AND SENT IT TO YOUR HOTEL BY EMAIL. DID YOU RECEIVE IT?

I'VE JUST BEEN GIVEN IT, BUT I HAVEN'T OPENED THE ENVELOPE YET.

PREPARE YOURSELF FOR AN UNPLEASANT SURPRISE...

KNOCK KNOCK

I'VE GIVEN YOU A BOTTLE OF SAUVIGNON WITH YOUR CHICKEN SANDWICHES.

THAT WILL BE PERFECT. THANK YOU.

!?!?

N° 134

(43)

file: //CIN.

45

DWIGHT COCHRANE?

YES.

↑ 🅿 Parking Lot Shuttles
Do... oor Vans-Hotel Courtesy Shuttles
...ntal Car Shuttle

↑ 🛄 Gates 50-59
↑ 🎫 Ticket Purchase
← 🛄 Baggage Claim
→ ARRIVALS

Baggage Sto
Medical Cli
Restrooms

IRS.*
FOLLOW US,
PLEASE.

*INTERNAL REVENUE SERVICE, THE US INCOME TAX OFFICE

HAVE YOU JUST ARRIVED FROM THE CAYMAN ISLANDS?

VIA MIAMI, YES. WHY?...

NO ENTRY

THIS WILL ONLY TAKE A FEW MINUTES, MR
COCHRANE. OR A FEW YEARS, DEPENDING.

PLEASE OPEN YOUR
SUITCASE.

I PROTEST
STRONGLY AGAINST...

ALL RIGHT,
PROTEST. AND
OPEN.

HEY, GO EASY!
THAT SUITCASE
COST ME OVER
$400...

IF THE INFORMATION
WE RECEIVED IS
INCORRECT, THE US
GOVERNMENT WILL
REIMBURSE YOU.

BINGO!

I... I DON'T UNDERSTAND...

WE DO. AT A GLANCE,
I'D SAY THERE MUST
BE   AROUND
$500,000
THERE.

AND YOU WERE
EVEN KIND
ENOUGH TO
LEAVE THE
CAYMAN TRUST
BANDS ON THE
MONEY. YOU'VE
SAVED US A LOT
OF WORK, MR
COCHRANE.

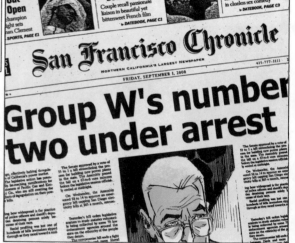

Out
Open
champion
ght sets
an Clement
SPORTS, PAGE E1

Couple recall passionate
liaison in beautiful yet
bittersweet French film
▶ DATEBOOK, PAGE C1

in clueless sex comedy
▶ DATEBOOK, PAGE C3

San Francisco Chronicle

NORTHERN CALIFORNIA'S LARGEST NEWSPAPER

415-777-1111

FRIDAY, SEPTEMBER 1, 2000

Group W's number
two under arrest

44

MR WINCH?

AGENT DAWSON AND AGENT BOXLEITNER, FBI DO YOU KNOW THIS PERSON?

?!

YES, HER NAME IS JULIET. WHAT'S HAPPENED TO HER?

YOU'RE THE ONE WHO'LL BE EXPLAINING THAT TO US, MR WINCH.

JULIET FERGUSON HAS FILED A COMPLAINT AGAINST YOU FOR KIDNAPPING, WITH INTERSTATE TRANSPORT, FALSE IMPRISONMENT, BODILY HARM AND SEXUAL ASSAULT. THE PLAINTIFF, AGED 17 YEARS OLD, IS A MINOR. THAT CONSTITUTES A FEDERAL CRIME, TO BE DEALT WITH BY THE SUPREME COURT.

??

YOU'RE UNDER ARREST, MR WINCH. PLEASE HOLD OUT YOUR HANDS. AGENT BOXLEITNER WILL READ YOU YOUR RIGHTS.

I DON'T GET IT. THIS IS A MISUNDERSTANDING.

WE'LL LEAVE THAT FOR THE DA TO DECIDE.

?!

!?

!....

FLZZ FLZZ FLZZ FLZZ FLZZ FLZZ FLZZ

45

HAHAHA! READING THE NEWS HAS NEVER BEEN SO MUCH FUN!

LADY, GENTLEMEN... I DRINK TO THE HEALTH OF OUR FRIEND LARGO WINCH AND TO THE SUCCESS OF "GOLDEN GATE," THE FIRST EPISODE OF WHICH HAS GONE EXACTLY ACCORDING TO PLAN.

AND I PROMISE YOU THAT THE SECOND EPISODE WILL NOT ONLY MAKE US RICHER BUT WILL BE A LOT MORE ENTERTAINING.

VAN HAMME & FRANCQ ©
99-00

END
OF THIS
EPISODE